Little Elephant and Hiccup Chuck

This book is dedicated to Braxton and Brynlei. May you always go after your dreams.

Author: Breanne Speer

Illustrated by: James Scofield

ISBN: 9781695032538

Each day Little Elephant wakes up excited to play hide-and-seek with her friends.

As she and her friends walk to the park, they listen to Grandpa Elephant tell the best stories about his childhood and life adventures.

One day Little Elephant was playing her best game of hide-and-seek ever, until she got the hiccups.

No matter how hard she tried to hide, her hiccups kept interrupting the game.

Little Elephant was underneath an umbrella at first, but when she hiccupped it went flying to the sky and Little Zebra could easily spot her.

Next, Little Elephant climbed into the swirling slide and stayed as quiet as she could. But it didn't take long for the sound of her hiccups to echo throughout the park.

Little Penguin followed the sound to the slide and when he peered into it, he found Little Elephant hiding. She was so embarrassed.

Finally, Little Elephant went to the top of an old tree and hid behind the leaves. But before she knew it, her hiccups made her bounce up and when she landed back down, all the leaves had gone.

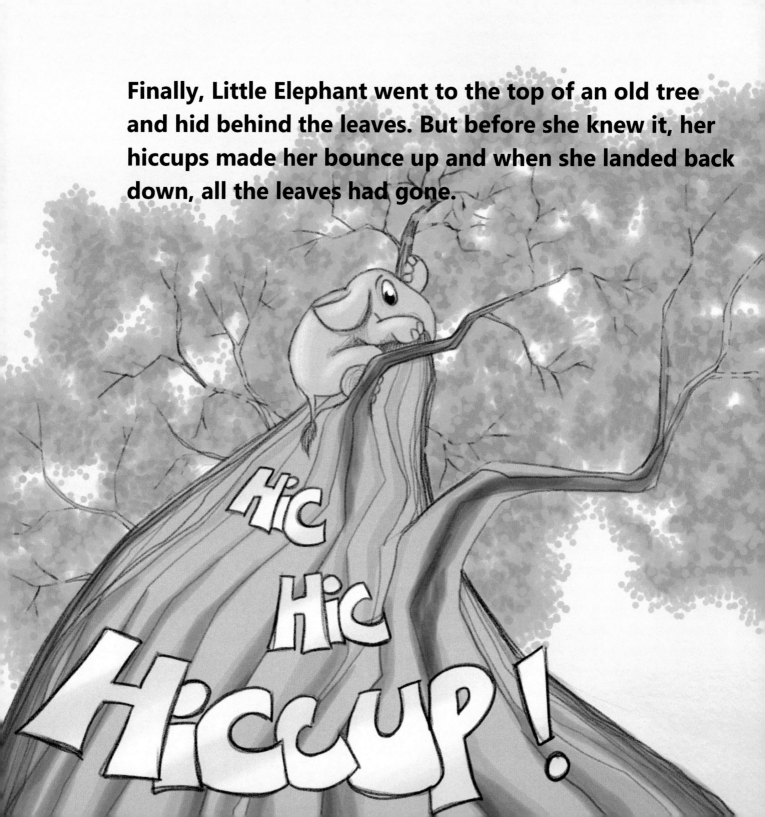

Little Monkey swung over and found Little Elephant sitting in the leafless tree.

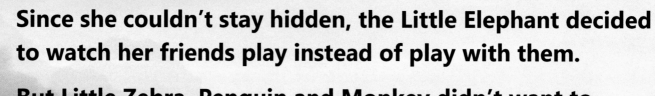

Since she couldn't stay hidden, the Little Elephant decided to watch her friends play instead of play with them.

But Little Zebra, Penguin and Monkey didn't want to play hide-and-seek without Little Elephant. They wanted to help her get rid of her hiccups. Together, they asked Grandpa Elephant how they could help their friend.

Grandpa Elephant told them a story about Hiccup Chuck, who lives in a bubble inside each of them.

The little animals had never heard about Hiccup Chuck but wanted to know more.

Grandpa Elephant explained that Hiccup Chuck sleeps all the time but, occasionally he will wake up. When Hiccup Chuck wakes up, he wants to play by jumping on his bed.

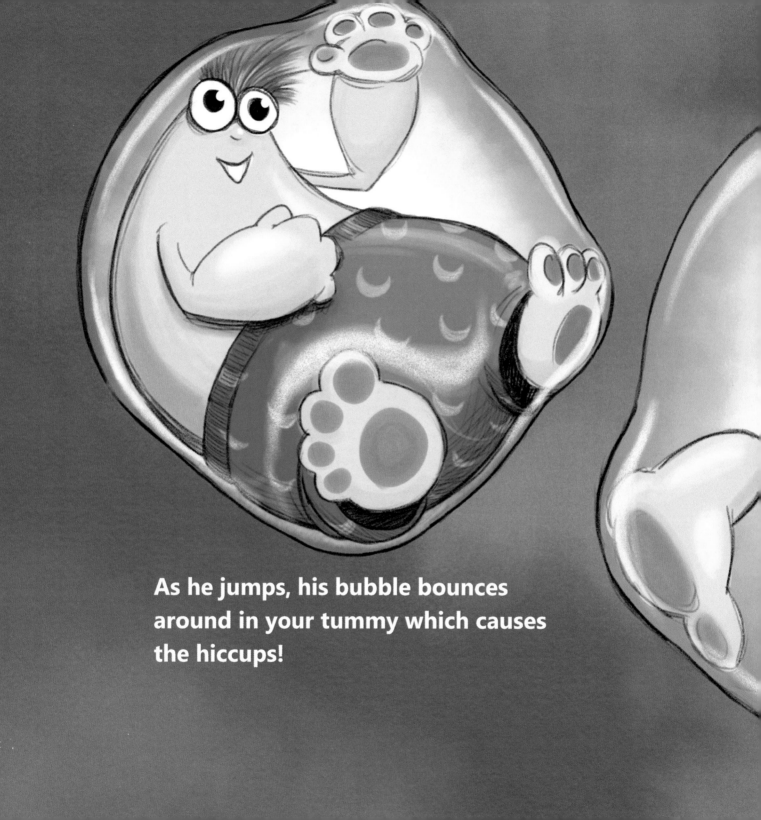

As he jumps, his bubble bounces around in your tummy which causes the hiccups!

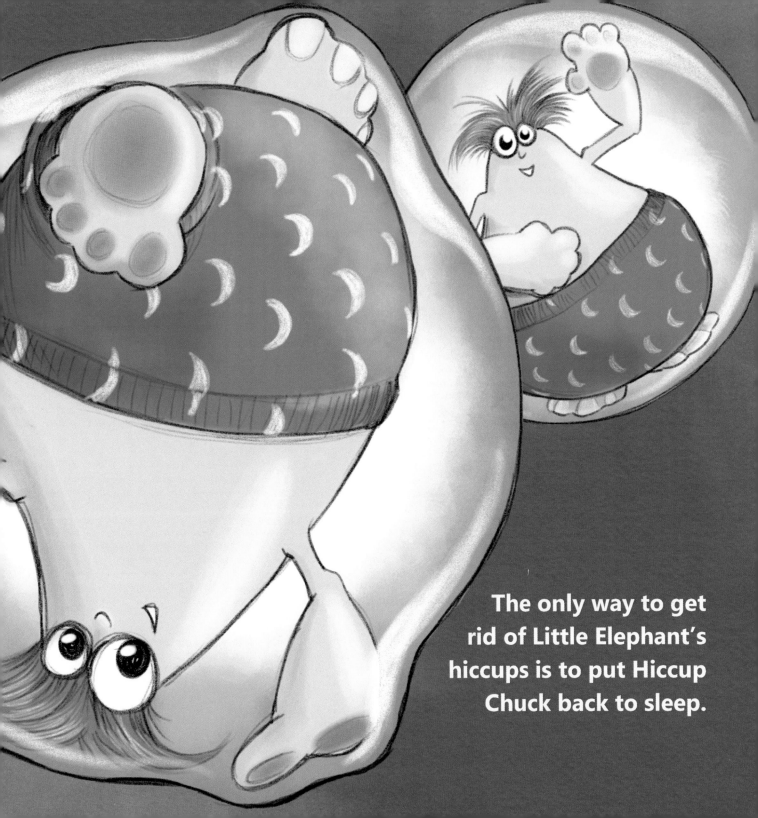

The only way to get rid of Little Elephant's hiccups is to put Hiccup Chuck back to sleep.

Grandpa Elephant taught the animals a special song. Hoping to help their friend, they all began singing with her:

...nuck, it's time for bed,

Lay down and rest your head,

Close your eyes and say goodnight,

As you snuggle in just right.

Moments later, Little Elephant cheered with excitement because her hiccups had gone away!

The little animals knew the hiccups would never keep them from playing hide-and-seek again.

She was so thankful to her friends and her Grandpa for their help.

Hide-and-Seek!

It's time to head home for the day and Grandpa Elephant needs your help finding all the little animals.

Color this page and see if you can find where all the friends are hiding.

The little animals had to put Hiccup Chuck back to sleep to help their friend, but here are some tips to try next time you get the hiccups!

Hold your breath and slowly let out the air!

Drink water quickly!

Have a friend or family member scare you!

Try to close your eyes and relax, just like Little Elephant had to!

Meet the author

Breanne Speer is a mother of two young children from the mid Michigan area and first time author of her children's book, "Little Elephant and Hiccup Chuck." This book highlights the importance of family, friendship and teamwork while adding a fun solution to a common problem.

You can find a lot more about Breanne's creative endeavors and ways to keep up with her latest projects at **breannespeer.wixsite.com/breannespeer**.

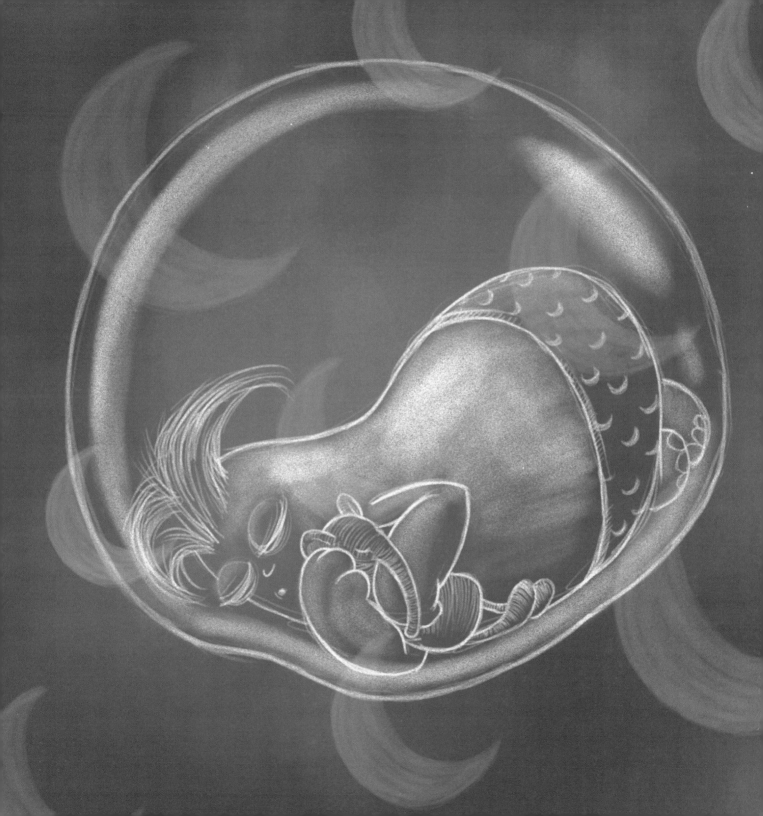

Made in the
USA
Columbia, SC